characters created by lauren chi

HELP!

I really mean it!

PUFFIN

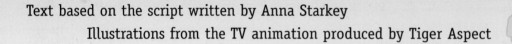

Text based on the script written by Anna Starkey

Illustrations from the TV animation produced by Tiger Aspect

PUFFIN BOOKS
Published by the Penguin Group: London, New York, Australia,
Canada, India, Ireland, New Zealand and South Africa
Penguin Books Ltd, Registered Offices: 80 Strand, London WC2R 0RL, England

puffinbooks.com

This edition published in Great Britain in Puffin Books 2010
1 3 5 7 9 8 6 4 2
Text and illustrations copyright © Lauren Child / Tiger Aspect Productions Limited, 2009
The Charlie and Lola Logo is a trademark of Lauren Child
All rights reserved. The moral right of the author/illustrator has been asserted
Manufactured in China
ISBN: 978-0-141-33493-6
This edition produced for The Book People Ltd,
Hall Wood Avenue, Haydock, St Helens, WA11 9UL

I have this little sister Lola.
She is small and very funny.
Today we are looking after Caspar,
Granny and Grandpa's cat.
Lola REALLY loves Caspar.

Lola says,
        "Look, Charlie!
Caspar is playing
        a game with us."

So I say,
        "Caspar is a cat.
                He might not like
        all of your games."

"He definitely
likes this one," says Lola.

Then Lola says,
"Lotta, did you know
        that Caspar is an
        actual tiger..."

"Oooh! Lola,
what are those noises?"
           asks Lotta.

Lola says,
           "I don't know.
But it's all right because
   we are with Caspar.

Oh...
   where's Caspar gone?"

And Lotta says, "Oh! Yes!
   Where's Caspar gone?"

Then Lola and Lotta shout,
   "HEEEELLLLPPPPP!"

Me and Marv run in
        and ask,
    "Are you all right?!"

And Lola says,
        "Yes, Charlie!
    Caspar was just going to
rescue me and Lotta
        from some tigers."

    So I say,
"Lola, you must ONLY
            call for help
if you REALLY mean it."

    And Lola says,
"Sorry, Charlie.
        We only said HELP
by accident."

Lotta says,
"It was very funny
        when we said HELP
and Charlie and Marv
            came running in."

And Lola asks,
"Do you think
        if we say help now,
they will come in
            again?"

"HELP! HELP!
        HELP! HELP!"

"What's the matter?!"
me and Marv ask.

And Lola says,
"Nothing, Charlie..."

So I say,
"Oh. I get it.
Very funny."

"We won't do it again,"
says Lola.

So I ask,
"Do you promise?"

And Lola says,
"We absolutely
do promise."

Later, Lotta says,
     "Look! Caspar
likes **dressing up**.

Do you think **cats**
like wearing **hats**?"

"Oh! I know they do,"
     says Lola.
"And they like going
for **carriage rides**, too.

Come on, Caspar.
     It's time for a **ride**."

"Caspar, where are you?"

"Are you here, Caspar?"
"Caspar! Where are you?"

"Caspar!
CASPAR!"

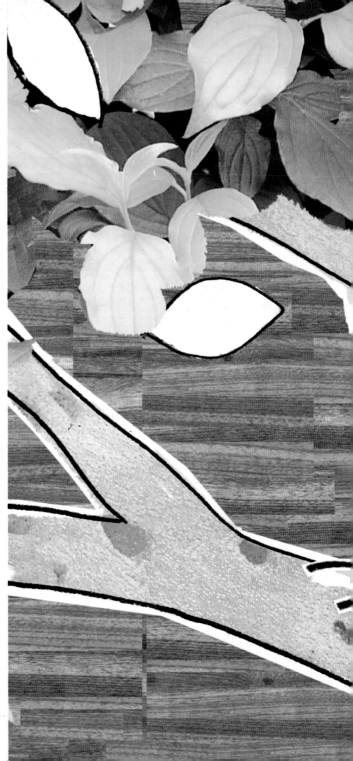

And I ask, "What is it
              this time, Lola?"

Lola says,
"Caspar's stuck
              right up in the sky,
and he's crying and his
              hat's gone all ᴡᴏɴᴋʏ!"

So I say,
              "Sorry, Lola.
It's not going to
              work this time."

And Lola says,
"But Charlie,
              we really, REALLY
need you to help..."

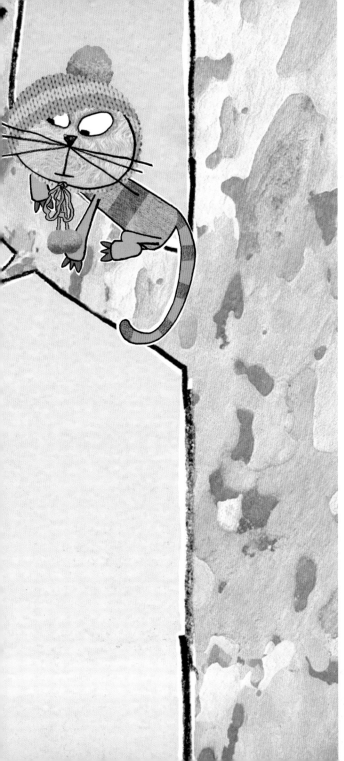

"Charlie and Marv
           don't believe me
so we've got to get Caspar
        down by ourselves.
Please come down, Caspar!"

And Lotta says, "PLEASE!"

Then Caspar climbs
       higher up the tree.

And Lola shouts,
           "Noooooo!
Charlie! HELP!"

Me and Marv run over
and Lola says,
"See? I did really need you."

And I say, "But I didn't
believe you because
you kept shouting HELP
when you didn't mean it."

Lola and Lotta say,
"Sorry, Charlie.
Sorry, Marv."

And I say,
"Look! Caspar has jumped
on to Marv's balcony!"

Then Marv says, "Err... Charlie,
why is that **cat** wearing a **hat**?"
So I say, "**Cats** don't like **hats**, Lola."
And Marv says,
"I would run away, too, if I had to wear a **hat** like that!"